Missy Mouse Meets THom Elf

Missy Mouse Meets THom Elf

Lake Harriet - Linden Hills
Minneapolis, Minnesota

Story and Photographs
by
Marilyn Clare

Missy Mouse Meets THom Elf
Lake Harriet - Linden Hills, Minneapolis, Minnesota

iUniverse books may be ordered through booksellers or by contacting:

iUniverse
1663 Liberty Drive
Bloomington, IN 47403
www.iuniverse.com
844-349-9409

ISBN: 978-1-4502-3294-4 (sc)
ISBN: 978-1-4502-3295-1 (e)

Print information available on the last page.

iUniverse rev. date: 11/30/2022

For my sister Jane
and
my dear friend Mary Jayne

Preface

The idea for this book began four years ago. Many thoughts were part of the process with lots of wondering if a fantasy-like fiction story coordinated with on location photographs, had merit. Somehow, the idea never faded; as an adult student in college, a full time working professional, and involvement with family, the passion for this book filled empty spaces of my schedule. One step at a time.

Savor each moment, be positive, turn thoughts to intent, to a purpose, and direct them for a beneficial end result. Blend elements of each thought to make whole-voice opinions, share experiences, and write stories. Thinking, an action, not physically seen, but wait a minute, in thought, we consider a deal, analyze or resolve issues, anticipate an event, intellectualize a theory, and make life choices. Mind, body, and action; it all works together to become action seen.

What about specifics of living where we perform in a certain capacity. The local newspaper publishes news of government issues, advertisements for products and service, theatre performances, and the classifieds! Buy, sell, and attain to a job (career) of choice. Join the health club, enter your child in sports activities and dance classes, volunteer for charity, run the marathon, take your dog for a walk, but don't forget the leash law; all filling the mind with enticements. They pervade and rein supreme; not one of these can be accomplished without thinking through, how, where, when and why. Today's function and functionary are supported by society, the work place, personal wants and need and technology.

Computer multi data programs, contained in a box, called an office cube, pressing keys on a keyboard; a computer's comprehensive collections of data and communications limit interacting with and hearing the voice of a person. Sunshine and blue sky were not seen beyond brick and mortar. With this, I won't analyze my thoughts; I am not cutting any deal, but reasoning with emotional significance. Think thoughts, dream dreams. Let them become reality. When the work day ended, Lake Harriet's lake edge surrounded me with green grass and fresh open air. Reminiscing, imagining; this kind of escape never lasted forever. But time was taken to explore pensive undisturbed thoughts and act upon them.

Searching the sunlight, a list was made and then photographing began one weekend at sunrise, then sunset and for several weeks thereafter the same. The best sunrises and sunsets were during September and October. Rain and inclement weather provided elements for fantasy-like 1800s appearance of several photographs Sunny day photos were taken by nine o'clock in the morning. *Missy Mouse Meets*

THom Elf emerged through, thought, intent, imagination, and with a history of having lived at Lake Harriet for over twenty years.

Change

1971, I was comfortable where I lived in Madison, Wisconsin and unaware change would come like a thief in the night; personal possessions were gathered into a big truck and driven, with my family, across the border to Minnesota. Everything was different; meeting new people, finding a new job; leaving a home that I liked where flowers were planted in a grassy yard landscaping. Wooded parks and farm land were within a few miles. Our new home, a small apartment on the fringe of Saint Paul was on a hill above a super highway. Windows remained closed because of heavy traffic noise. I took deep breaths; anxiousness loomed in search for "home." We moved again from the small apartment to a duplex, but train tracks were at our back door. The landlord assured us a train rarely came through. On the contrary, it woke us the first night and scared our wits. A house in Spring Lake Park, one year later, was neither the right place nor the wrong place.

1980, wondering, was there anywhere in the Twin Cities that represented home, as I remember, before moving to Saint Paul. A friend at my job spoke of Lake Calhoun and Lake Harriet. Acknowledging her invitation; it had been a long time that there was someone who supported feelings and shared mutual affections of persons, places or things. My daughters, Michelle and Margo liked spending a day at the beach; I packed a picnic and drove to Lake Calhoun, parked my car at the water's edge; my friend had told me that we were spending the day at a special part of the Twin Cities. Gazing at the lake and looking across; a grove of trees hid sky scraping condominiums, wind surfing sails of red, yellow, blue and green skimmed the water; it was a place of ideal beauty. She was right. Finding my friend, placing blankets beneath a giant Maple tree, the sun shone brilliant. Adults walking the path, interacting with their children, playing a game of Frisbee or throwing a wood stick for their pet dog to retrieve from the water, being with my children and playing with them; there was nowhere like this where we used to live overlooking the highway in Saint Paul or in Spring Lake Park. Quiet and peaceful, conversation and laughter, watching the water's flow and the changing sun's reflection, minutes turned to hours, the lake's beach, big trees, houses that held stories of old, I loved this community. My friend told me that Lake Harriet was within a few blocks; taking the time to visit before heading to Spring Lake Park, that day was the beginning of many return trips. Back then, the drive from north Minneapolis to the lakes was like a mini vacation. 1981 we moved to Lake Harriet and my children attended Washburn Grade School and graduated from Southwest High School.

A park, a lake, and nature within the city, we were at home.

Photographs show Lake Harriet my way or rather than indicating that I am one up on you, I am one with you. There was something about Lake Harriet that delighted me beyond measure. You have visited Lake Harriet, and then maybe you haven't. But in showing you lake views and plants and trees and tall grasses through the lenses of my eyes, you will remember the park and if you have never been to Lake Harriet, you will share my experiences within these pages. No villains exist at Lake Harriet, but one hero, an elf, exists in heart and mind. Lake Harriet's elf house will be revealed in the story. From the characters point of view, I share an adventure of realism and of truth and of fiction, but how much fiction based on truth? You decide. In addition, have you ever walked a path at a favorite park or wooded area and wondered how creatures of nature see their environment? What does their world look like from the ground up?

I chose to live at Lake Harriet. My journey did not begin here, but it ended here, not in finality of life experiences, but with new experiences; change opened perceptions for goals, especially one that had been a life-long dream. I've walked Lake Harriet's path, my children and grandchildren played here. I speculated curiosity and wondered the possibility of writing stories, Thoughts turned reality, *Missy Mouse Meets THom Elf* imaginary idea evolved. Many first time experiences were a part of living at Lake Harriet, planning the next research project for family history; following the Olympic Games on television, and deciding to become an Augsburg Weekend College student. *Missy Mouse Meets THom Elf* was a fluke. One day in the year 2006, at a course session end, my English Expository Writing instructor, Professor Harkness, gave us an assignment to write a fable.

"Now I don't mean for any of you to be exact with format, you don't need to be particular, but write a fable, just for fun. The exercise of writing's importance was in learning the skill. You have fifteen minutes until class dismisses, you may get your pens in motion now, but you may finish this project in your spare time; I want you to hand in your fable next week at class," he said.

I looked at my classmate, Rich, seated next to me.

"I don't write children's stories, what on earth am I going to write?" Together we laughed.

Expository writing textbook was based on theories of writing through elements of nature. The main goal of the textbook showed writing examples through symbolic relationships. One was a story about climbing a mountain; another, becoming one with nature. Each was a unique perspective to writing, but the question, where in a city do we find nature was asked as part of writing processes. Of course, Lake Harriet came to mind. Hesitation prevented writing, remember, I had fifteen minutes. Rich and I laughed to cause a disturbance. Writing a fable was nowhere in the mix of what I believed our course instructor would teach. I stared at the blank paper in front of me, pen in hand; I wrote nothing. Seeing an article in Southwest Journal, Lake Harriet neighborhood newspaper, about the elf house; and my friend, Mary Jayne, who lived at Lake Harriet introduced my children and me to the elf house. Maybe a fable could be written about the elf. That sure was a kid thing.

"Don't forget that you need more than one character," our instructor's voice directed.

All in the class voiced an opinion in unison, none of which was clear.

"Stretch your capability, your mind, extend your vocabulary, emphasize sentence structure, and let your imagination form mental images and don't be afraid to write what first comes to your mind. I expect this of you." Our instructor exhorted.

Oh, gosh, now what? More than one character, and then all of a sudden I had an additional name. My name begins with the letter M, I thought, my daughter's names begin with the letter M and our pet kitty's name begins with the letter M. In loving gesture their names were preceded with Missy when we were playful; it was Missy Michelle and Missy Margo and Missy Muffy Peeper Cat. The Lake Harriet elf's interacting character was named before class end, Missy Mouse. In wooded areas there are wood mice or field mice; this was all I wrote and thought through by the time class ended. Somewhere between the classroom and Lake Harriet the idea for *Missy Mouse Meets THom Elf* story was born.

Imagination, put to the test, saw a big picture. Words on paper described Lake Harriet, but the lake views, flowers and bushes, tall trees and sail boats, and buildings where music groups played and food was served and the Trolley Museum gave rides; no words on paper described the elf house or the area in detail, but adding graphics and photos would. I then solicited my granddaughter, Korie, who was nine years old, to pencil draw her interpretation of the elf and Missy Mouse.

My daughter, Margo, joined me on a sunny day with her camera. After all, she grew up here and wanted to be a part of this project. The ground up, let's take pictures from the ground up. Hands, knees, on the ground, if you were a mouse what would the mouse see? If you were an elf, what would an elf see? Animated and assured, from the ground up, people watched us; we were unusual in photographing a certain world view. Korie drew a wagon full of furniture. Missy Mouse was moving to Thom Elf house, she didn't know her journey was to make her home at his house, or that her journey was to begin at a purple house, but I did.

Korie's pencil drawings, scanned into Adobe Photo Shop and Microsoft Picture Express were given animation. I continued with photographing Lake Harriet and finalizing the manuscript. *Missy Mouse Meets THom Elf* doesn't give in to forms of misfortune, but success in accomplishment in finding a new home. Share with me one day in the process below:

Thursday, July 5, 2007 6:31:09 AM

I formatted Missy Mouse photographs and graphics all afternoon until eleven o'clock in the evening yesterday. I stopped, though, to go to the park for an ice cream cone. Bluegrass music was playing at the Band Shell. However, the bugs were bigger than the music, I stayed long enough to finish my ice cream and then I left for home.

Most of my day was spent with the pictures and then setting them on a page. But do you think I can coordinate the pictures with my visual and put them to paper so story and photos show what I see in my head! No! By last night, I couldn't believe I had anything workable, including my story. Missy Mouse idea is difficult.

Finally, though I took it all away from Microsoft Word and copied photos and story to Adobe Power Point. Now, it makes much better sense. Make an outline. Walk the area at Lake Harriet again and continue believing how much fun the idea, especially for a book, has become. Leaving things to the imagination is amusing and challenging. Realizing the ideas for the concept is about things that kids and adults talk about. Like the feather being on the ground in one photo and in her ribbon in the next photo. That's fun. Think about the conversations kids could have about finding things on the ground and picking them up as if they were some kind of treasure in the story. That's what Missy Mouse did when she found the feather. Pictures are worth more than words or leads to other stories that kids and adults can talk about by using their imaginations. Children's books are vehicles for talking about things more than they are used for teaching reading. Keep the flow going. Fantasy and reality mixed. Anxiety of moving and making new friends and Missy Mouse shows this by example of moving from a grand house to a hole in a tree. Kids don't understand downsizing but there can be a subtle message, in the adults reading interpretation, with the kids, that it doesn't take material things to be happy and leave things to the imagination.

A child's story, a coffee table picture book of Lake Harriet; join me in the journey of *Missy Mouse Meets THom Elf.*

Acknowledgements

Thank You

Graphics by

Without the encouragement of my Augsburg college professors, the idea for this book would have never happened. Through several English courses, I began to see a broad world view. Something wonderful happened and a story emerged through an imagination I did not know I had. Photographing Lake Harriet was like a hobby that had usefulness beyond personal entertainment. In the midst, I met people who assisted my efforts in thought, word, and deed.

Como-Harriet Streetcar Line

The Minnesota Streetcar Museum

www.trolleyride.org

Scott Heiderich – Director and Treasurer, assisted my safety when photographing the trolley.

My daughter, Margo, assisted with photographs because she thought it might be fun. The morning she arrived was sunny and bright and photographs are of the rose garden, the result of these photos, when seen by my sister Jane; she gave me a camera and I continued the photo process.

In addition, numerous conversations were held among friends and neighbors of Linden Hills. Absorbed in their smiles and their encouragement, this book idea continued. There were people who spoke to me with curiosity when I was photographing the lake and who then gave me ideas for locations.

A neighbor permitted photos of their yard with fantasy-like ceramics to mimic elfin and fairytale flowers and greenery.

I am deeply grateful for everyone's collaboration.

Further explanations are at the beginning of the story.

A special thanks to my sister who gave input and helped sort ideas and said, "The idea for this story is a great example of complexities of life."

All In A Day

There was no advantage to ponder the next step. One day it came swift like a fluke of fortune pouring from a magic box when its lid flew ajar. Happenchance might not be per chance, but with purposeful intent and soon you will know through visions of "once upon a time."

There was a young woman who triflingly courted memories of one thing or another. Thinking, daydreaming; stopping everything that needed attention, her daydreaming was to ask the question; was it true that all at Lake Harriet in Linden Hills lived happily ever after?

An unusual circumstance persisted; passionate feelings toward nature's abundance and goodness were not accidental. When sunrise accented, some sort of energy propelled her against resistance of being contained within the house. Through an open window, springtime air, by virtue of its potency, drew her to where trees were leafing, flowers were budding, and where people, who were compelled the same as her were gathered. She had spent winter days in the house. Temptation overcame her. She left every "must do," unlatched the door, and entered into a place of solitude. She went for a walk!

Warm breezes passed over her face like a whiff of pure splendor. Obliterating thoughts of customary obligations for family, career, and extra activities, she looked toward the sky at the treetops and then down upon the cemented walkway where she stepped. What contradiction was this to stifle growth of grass and natural vegetations beneath an overlay of hardened man-made concrete, when above, the treetops beckoned release from all sense of duty with their swaying branches and green seedling leaves? Steadied and protected from the ground's unevenness; stone like material had a purpose, she supposed. Approaching the fenced gateway, bright color crimson and gold ignited the sky like flames of fire on the horizon. The sun's rays were burning the morning dew and with it, thoughts of responsibilities dissipated.

Walking where nature dictated tranquility, soon she was distanced from pending concerns. And unlike happenchance, calculated and intentional; her point of full departure was around the bend.

Forty Second Street, located at the intersection of Broadway and Time's Square in New York City and the topic for *Forty Second Street*, the movie, which told of its theaters; in Linden Hills, Forty Second Street, she knew, had not much to do about anything; no hoopla, no recognition, but led her to enchantments of many possibilities. Well, maybe, the idea of escape to the lake, with trees and flowers, birds, little ground animals, and baby fish swimming at the shoreline, fantasy thoughts took over. She stopped at a steep decline where the street and the golden sunrise met on Forty Second Street. The water and charm of sail boats and painted buildings and more trees and flowers was a place of transformation. She became one with nature. If she hurried, she'd be at the water's edge in a blink. Aware that those sensations of exhilaration were not hers alone, but stupendous persons existed at Lake Harriet in Linden Hills and they walked and ran by her.

Walk, walking, sunbeams burst as crystalline upon the lake; all things that required her concentration and focus had been left back there.

Sandy lake shores were enticing with approaching summer's warm air. Frolicking where there was whimsy, impatient to wait and barefoot, in sweeping motion, water spewed her skirt hem. Sail boats were anchored; their white sails would rise to the sky soon and she remembered how they filled the lake with their grandeur. Men, women, and children had cast fishing lines from the docks. Fishing boats scaled the water. The Rose Garden and The Japanese Garden beckoned to stroll through and at their perimeter, with easel and canvas, artists will paint petals of red, yellow, orange, white, and trees of ornate structures with leaves of green and bows that bend to the ground. Dawdling and lingering, nothing seemed urgent. Cupping her shoulders, putting her arms to her chest, taking a deep, deep breath; embracing color and texture of the landscape and the water's tranquility; dreamy thoughts spread throughout all parts of her. Lake Harriet, Linden Hills, a special place; squirrels scampering, chirping birds flying overhead, glowing was the mid-day sun, dimming the light for a minute were fluffy clouds. Everyone said, "Hello." The essence of nature was reason for her to fancy Lake Harriet.

Lingering with a cup of coffee at the café, breezes sent a new message of peacefulness, pondering; moving waters bouncing off the rocky edge; momma ducks feeding their ducklings, imaginings of illusive stories and poetry, remembering summers past when oils flowed on artist's canvas with fluid brush strokes; their scenes unaffected by meandering men women and children. A yard garden; ceramic elfins, trolls, a turtle, a mushroom, and lily flowers of scarlet, daffodils of yellow and Forget-Me Not of blue; one block from the café; she would go home that way.

Residents and visitors watched when the soil was turned for the Japanese Garden and they watched when bushes and flowers and trees were planted with the restoration of the Lake Harriet Band Shell and recreational buildings and when workers painted tan over their original blue. They watched when rocks were piled along the water's shores. Change; the things of the world change, at work, at home, in cities, and communities, but memories remain; she recalled impressions of what was, including one day, today will be a memory.

> A window is just a window. A window of glass and frame
> of wood viewed from inside out or outside in, matters not.
> A window is just a window.

And so too, a little door was attached at the base of a tree where nature designed a knot, a hole of darkness, or a house to reside? Inquisitive, a door was placed over the hole to look like the entry of a fortress, a castle, a cottage, or whatever an imagination decided. Children watched; men and women watched and waited, but there was no action to see, the door appeared, disappeared, and then reappeared. Who placed the door? Who took the door? A phantom hammer nailed the door to the tree? Or a phantom used a hammer and nailed the door to the tree, covering the dark hole. By power of inventiveness it was whatever visitors wanted it to be, and from it, an illusory figure was born. An elfin. Tom an ordinary name or one impish and mischievous, THom? He's real in the minds and hearts of all who visit Lake Harriet, every day, to this day. A lively character that THom! Romping in merriment, skipping and nimbly dancing; his gaiety; would be, could be, and is. Known only through notions of supposing, his years of experience gave him personality, his form, his stature, and build; although it's been asked, "What do you really look like, THom? His last name might be Elf.

And she remained pensive.

Missy Mouse' Journey

Missy Mouse lolled on the sill of the upstairs bedroom window every day. The sun, warm in the corner behind the ruffled curtain; she rested her head on her paw; she fell asleep. This morning was quiet.

But Mistress had a day off from work and was about her business. Dusting the furniture, sweeping the floor; the sun shone bright; Mistress sang songs and delighted in the sunrise. Master was leaving for work.

"I'll bring the kittens home; hold supper until I arrive! I'll call you!"

Slamming the door, he darted to his car.

"I can hardly wait!" Mistress yelled excitement.

Master and Mistress owned a purple house near Lake Harriet. They found kittens through a classified ad in the newspaper. Missy Mouse awakened. When no one was in the kitchen, climbing the cabinets in search of food and eating crumbs from the floor, under the table, was Missy Mouse' favorite pastime.

Mistress played loud radio music and danced around the dining room table. Perplexed by the merrymaking, Missy Mouse tripped downstairs wondering about the commotion.

Later that day, a moment of fussing, a moment of ballyhoo, the front door flung wide open. Master was home.

"Grab the door! Take the box! I have one more box!" Master turned and hurried to his car.

Missy Mouse scurried to the kitchen and crawled into the cabinet beneath the sink. Bottles and containers hid her. What's in the boxes? She thinks. Big feet masked her view. Her nostrils twitched. Something in the boxes rustled.

She listened…

Quiet …

No one was at home…

She popped through the open cabinet door, scampered to the doorway that led to the living room…

OH NO, A CAT!

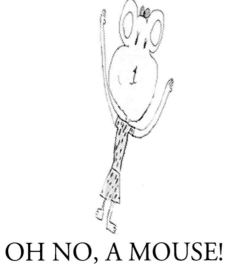

OH NO, A MOUSE!

Scared Missy Mouse slid and slipped, wobbled and ran, curled into a ball, gyrated across the wood floor, bumped against the stair well, and hastened up each step. She landed on the sill of the bedroom window in the corner behind the ruffled curtain. Crouched; she quivered and moved not. All through the night.

The next morning, hungry, thirsty; tired; Missy Mouse loaded her things into a wagon. A momma cat, three kittens, and Missy Mouse must not live in the same purple house.

At the picket gate, she looked left, right, and then straight ahead. She wondered, which way should she go.

Puzzled, but assured, holding the wagon's handle, powering it alone, leaving the comforts of the sunny window sill; she remembered food crumbs were on the kitchen floor. But the cat was resting by the table leg. She went straight ahead.

And the wagon rolled down the hill...

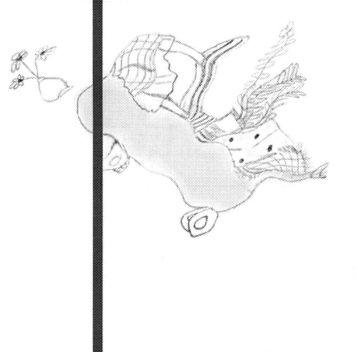

and landed in a clump of grass

Missy Mouse fell asleep…

Under a Sunflower petal

Awakened, the sun's heat at her back,
Missy Mouse wondered where was she?

"Here are your flowers," the elfin said.

Missy Mouse was a wood mouse and was set apart from all other tan-gray wood mice because of her white face. She grabbed the handle of her wagon, which way should she go?

And then...

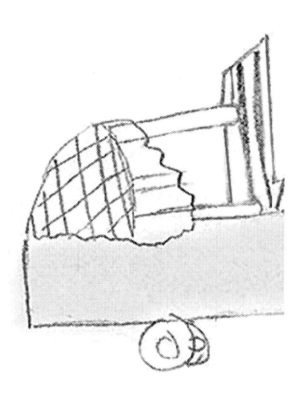

Screech!

Far below a big machine moved on wheels.

Screech!

Her ears bristled. Peering through the fence, she maneuvered her wagon away and wondered which way to go.

At The Trolley

At The Lake

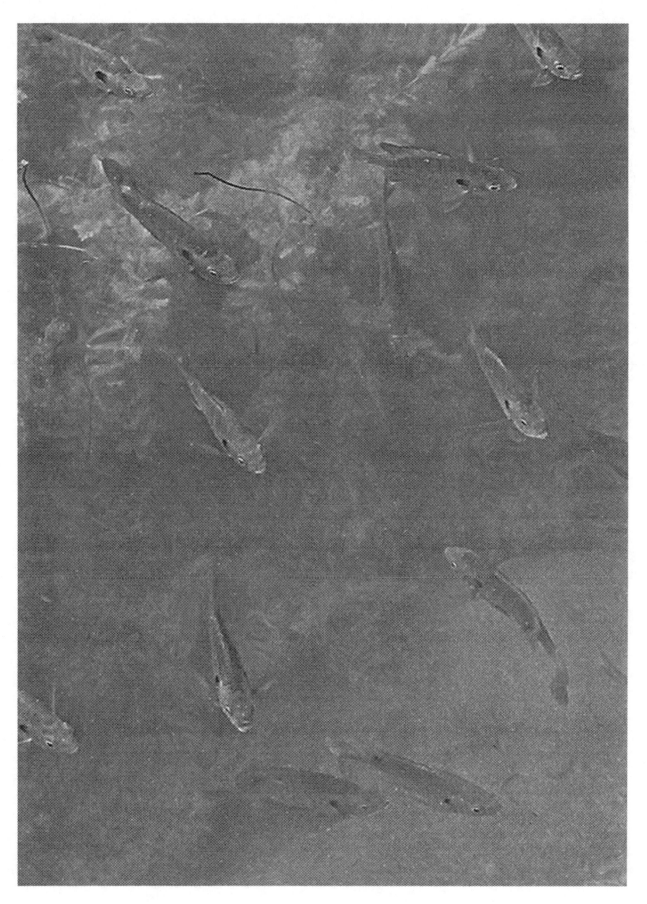

At The Rose Garden

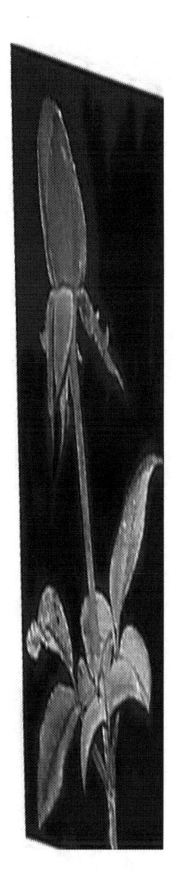

At The Japanese Garden

Afternoon shadows beneath winding branches of the sycamore tree, a Japanese Garden, a favorite place to rest and dream of tomorrow, and give thankfulness for today.

In the shadows, beneath the winding branches away from the sun's heat, flowers cluster near the ground and green shrubbery sends sweet aromas into the air.

Shadows lay designs upon velvety grasses as if painted by a master, black upon green, variegated where the sun's light glows between winding branches of the sycamore tree.

The season knows color, but the shadows hold mystery like a story of old lurking within winding branches of the sycamore tree, sultry, close, and moist.

Do I linger in this favorite place? A photograph gives me rest in the shadows of the winding branches, this sycamore tree, turning pages, a new dream begins.

On the path to her new home

A house! She finds a house!

A dilemma.

How does she get in?

Digging a hole to get into the tree house, crouching tight to the ground; Swishing sounds did not distract her, but skimming her side were big feet.

The elfin watched.

THOm
eLf
lives here

Missy Mouse moved in.

The next day, I wish there were neighbors, she thinks. Master and Mistress were company, even if they did not talk to me; she had conversations with herself.

"Ouch, someone stepped on my tail!" She exclaimed. She lost her composure and circled around and around and around, trying to catch her tail.

"Big feet do not know that I live here." She mumbled.

Scurry hurry, rush, hurry. She slipped through the hole. Inside, dark and cold; the rush quieted, she opened the tree house door to the outside. Then shut it again and sat down. She rested.

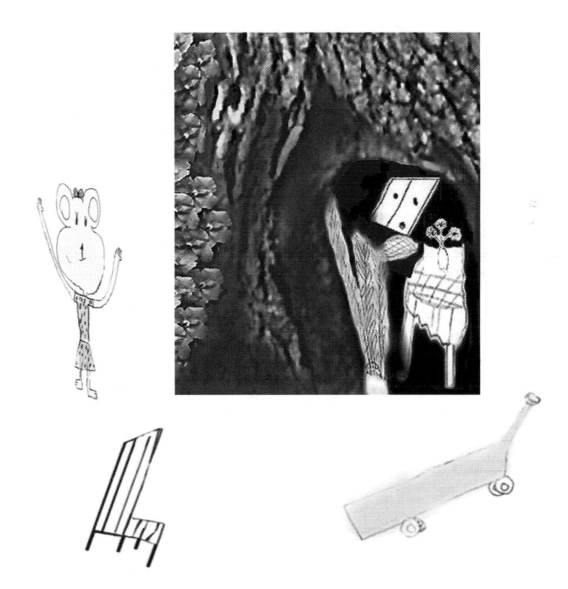

One day Missy Mouse went into the trail of big feet to find some food.

"It's risky business to live by this lake where big feet walk from early morning to late at night," she said.

Not able to see above the soles of their shoes, she didn't know people were part of the big feet. She fled to her little house in the tree for a nap.

Tromping, stomping, she was awakened and went outside.

Wiggling her way through big feet, she picked up a brown paper bag left by her house and gathered seeds for dinner. The bag was heavy.

"If only I had a friend to help me carry the seeds, I'd share them," she said, but no one could hear her.

Sniff, snort, sniff, and sniff.

"Oh no! There's that lapped-mouthed, licking, sneaking around dog again. He was here last night. He doesn't know I am here. Dog, go away! You trampled my flowers. You are a sniffing curious dog! I am a mouse and no one knows my purpose. I eat all the seeds that are scattered by the lake where big feet walk," she charges after him.

Persnickety, Missy Mouse kept everything in perfect order at the purple house. There was a warm window sill where she slept in the sun, water beneath the sink, food crumbs under the kitchen table. Chasing a dog that ran off with her door was not a good life.

"Dog!, Dog!" Missy Mouse' voice was heard from the tree house to the lake.

"Snarling, growling. Dog thinks it's a bone to chew." Missy Mouse whimpers.

"You heisted my door because of your self-interest and ran off. You might lose friends that way," said she.

Missy Mouse, zigzagging through prickly bushes; her ribbon and feather fell to the ground.

Stopping to rest, the elfin came light and quick. Holding the tree house door, bowing and gesturing, he stood at her side. He reached to give her the door. She wondered, who can this person be?

"Thank you." Missy Mouse was not sure what to make of it.

"You're welcome; my name is THom Elf," said he.

He then spoke of wind and weather and that the door must be reattached somehow.

As the story goes, the sun set on the horizon of her first day; THom Elf never revealed that she moved into his house. She wandered into tall grasses and continued the risky business in search of seeds. No longer did she think of the purple house, Master or Mistress, food crumbs beneath the table in the kitchen, or the cat and kittens that chased away. She forgot the sunny window sill and where she slept behind the ruffled curtains.

THE END

Photo Credits in Order of Sequence by Page

Graphics: Korie Manley

Cover: Lake Harriet Band Shell, café and concessions, recreation area, picnic shelter, *Wheel Fun Rentals, and* Lake Harriet Yacht Club

1. Como-Harriet Streetcar Line, Lake Harriet, and Elf House – black and white

2. Rocks along the shore of Lake Harriet near the picnic shelter. A man caught a big fish wile photographing.

3. Tree on the walking path on a rainy day

4 & 5. Beyond the rocks along the shore; a few yards

6. A bend on the path toward the Elf House

7 &
8. Trees on the path toward the Elf House

9. Overlooking the lake to the side of the **Band Shell**

10. Same as "Cover"

11. Through the stage window of the Band Shell

12. Inside the snack shop café ceiling

13. Outside through the stage window of the Band Shell

14. House called the Purple House

15. Missy Mouse and Cat

16. Purple House and wagon

17 &
18. Neighborhood fantasy garden

19.-
22. Como-Harriet Streetcar Line

23-
25. Lakc Harrict views

26. Actual fishes swimming at shoreline.

27. Lake Harriet view

28. Stored Canoes at the shoreline

29. Rose Garden

30 &
31. Japanese Garden

32. On the trail toward the Elf House

33. The bridge and finding a feather

34. Feeding the ducks and fishing dock

35. Elf House

36. Feet walking the path

37. Dog tracks in the sand at the beach

38 &
39. Deck chair at Lake Harriet Beach

40 &
41. Tree at Lake Harriet

42. Cover Back: Como-Harriet Streetcar Line, Lake Harriet, and Elf House –
    Color

Printed in the United States
by Baker & Taylor Publisher Services